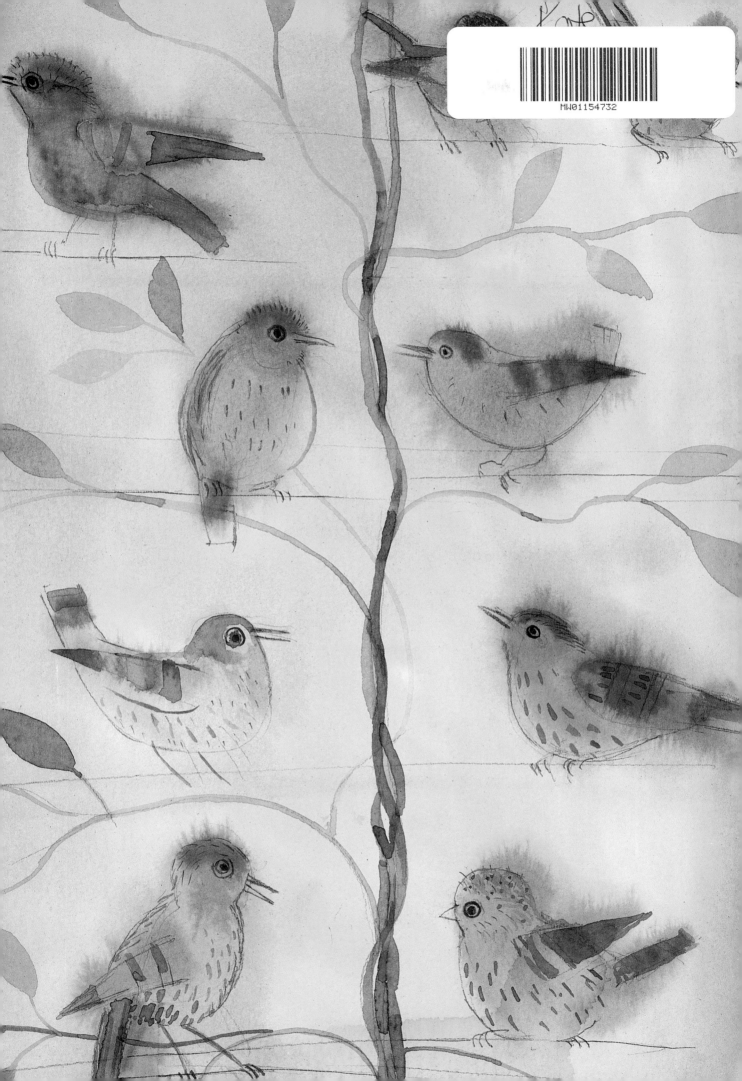

A story by
JEANNE PEREGO

Illustrated by
DONATA DAL MOLIN CASAGRANDE

Translated by
DARIA KISSEL

Max and Benedict

A Bird's Eye View of the Pope's Daily Life

Foreword by
FATHER DAMIANO MARZOTTO
Official of the Congregation for the Doctrine of the Faith

Afterword by
FULVIO FRATICELLI
Scientific Director, Biopark of Rome Foundation

IGNATIUS PRESS   SAN FRANCISCO

Original Italian edition:
Max e Benedetto: Un passero solitario racconta la giornata del Papa

Layout: Monica Faccini
Cover artwork: Giuliano Dinon

ISBN 978-1-58617-407-1

Manufactured by Friesens Corporation
Manufactured in Altona, Manitoba, Canada
In September 2009, Job number 48895

Foreword

The Emperor Nero enjoyed playing war games at sea, so near the Tiber River he ordered the construction of a circus, which he flooded with water from a canal and used to recreate naval battles with small ships.

One day a huge fire broke out in Rome, and the Christians were accused of setting it. Many Christians were taken to Nero's circus and martyred there. Saint Peter also died during that persecution. When his friends were able to retrieve his body, they decided to bury him in a nearby cemetery on the Vatican hill. From that day on, more and more pilgrims came to pray over his tomb, and they would leave written invocations on an adjacent wall.

Over time, first a small monument and then a church were built on the site. Ultimately, subsequent popes decided to create their residence there, and the apostolic palace was built. When people walk through Saint Peter's Square, they look up and see, high above the colonnade surrounding the square, a large building with two windows lit until very late at night.

They say, "That's where the Pope lives. The windows are lit, which means the Pope is working." But what is the Pope's job? What does he do all day long? This book was created to answer these questions, and I am grateful to the author for giving us a respectful yet compelling glimpse of the daily life of Saint Peter's successor.

I personally had the joy of working for twenty-three years with Joseph Cardinal Ratzinger, before he was elected Pope Benedict XVI, when he was the Prefect of the Congregation for the Doctrine of the Faith. He was a tireless worker, but, above all, he was an amiable and cordial person. I hope this book will help everyone, but especially children, become more familiar with the Pope through this story about his daily life told by a little bird nesting on the dome of Saint Peter's Basilica. Readers will have a chance to discover the effort but also the joy with which the Pope strives to follow in the footsteps of Saint Peter, who is buried underneath that dome, right at the foot of the Vatican hill. Jesus entrusted Saint Peter and his successors with the Church so they could guide her, like a small boat, through the waves of history, fraught with always new difficulties and dangers, towards the Lord, who awaits us on the beach. We trust in the steadfast hand of the Pope, but we also know that he counts on our prayers. I hope this book will warm our hearts and renew our promise always to remember the Holy Father in our prayers.

Father Damiano Marzotto

Rome, January 2, 2009

Max and Benedict

Tweet! Tweet! Chirrrr!! Hi! I'm Max! Who are you? I'm a blue rock-thrush who likes to live where it isn't too cold.

I decided to call myself Max because no one ever thinks of giving names to the birds soaring in the sky.

The first time I said I wanted a name, I was about your age. My brothers started teasing me: "What will you do with a name?"

"Who has to call you?"

What do you mean, "Who has to call you?!?" I wanted a name for *myself*, not because I wanted someone to call me! I just didn't want to be an ordinary rock-thrush. But it was useless talking to the two of them: they aren't very bright. The only things that mattered to them were the berries and bugs that Dad brought us to eat. All they ever thought of was food, food, food. Once, when they were fighting over a berry, they even knocked me out of the nest! Fortunately, Mom caught me in mid-air. Otherwise, I would have been in *big* trouble.

I started looking for a name that suited me when I left the family nest, after lots of flying lessons with Dad. I was just over a month old, but for a rock-thrush, that means being almost all grown up.

I searched for a name as I flew over roads, homes, and gardens, and I listened to the names people gave their horses, dogs, and cats. I didn't like any of them, unfortunately. Can you imagine a rock-thrust being called Fido, Caracalla, or Socks?

By the way, where do you humans get such ridiculous ideas like calling a cat "Socks"? If I were that cat, I would have already left home. We animals have our dignity, too!

I racked my brain for days trying to find a name as I flew about town. I observed what was happening around me. I listened to people in their homes and the sounds of their words floating in the breeze, but there was nothing that suited me.

Finally, one day, my eye caught some words that you see here and there in the place where I decided to live: the dome on Saint Peter's Basilica, a huge pudding-shaped building that I leave only when I go hunting for something yummy to eat or when I set off to explore the area.

I realized that almost all of the phrases had the same two words: PONT.MAX. They had to be two *very important* words, since they were everywhere!

"Pont.Max., Pont.Max.", I kept repeating.

I wasn't keen on Pont, but I really liked Max.

"That's my name!" I said. "Max!"

"Max! Max! Max! I like the sound of it!"

Max is a short, strong name as quick as a brisk flap of the wings.

That's how Max became my name.

I'm not the only bird that has decided to live on Saint Peter's dome. There are also chubby pigeons, kestrels, sparrows, jackdaws, and a few white wagtails. At the start of winter, several black redstarts arrive, leaving the cold mountain weather behind them. There's even an elegant wall-creeper, which looks like a big butterfly when it flies.

The dome is like a large apartment building, and the residents here differ in appearance and personality. Some are bossy; others are friendlier. Some are nice, but some are not. Anyway, we all live together without too many problems. Each has his own space and his own behavior, and we all respect each other. It's really not that hard: it just takes a little effort.

If you look up at the dome, you'll see me: I'm the one on top, high above all the others. That's a little thing of mine: I like to perch there, all by myself, and gaze down at the world.

That's why they say I'm a sad, shy loner.

I might be shy, but I'm not sad at all! I'm a cheerful, happy little bird. When I'm in love, I like to sing out loud, and I have fun soaring and quickly diving through the air. But I don't like others around: I feel comfortable only when I can fly and watch things all by myself.

From my favorite perch, I carefully observe everything that happens in this part of town, which is a city inside a city. It's called the Vatican. I'm fascinated by all the hustle and bustle there.

But there is *one* person in particular who intrigues me: Pope Benedict XVI.

To me, he's just Benedict. Every time he comes to the window, the people in the square always cheer and call out his name in Italian:

"Be-ne-det-to, Be-ne-det-to!"

I've been observing him ever since I came to live on the dome.

I'm so fascinated by him that I often fly to one of the windowsills of his study where he works, just to see what he's doing.

I think he has seen me: if I start singing, he removes his gold-rimmed reading glasses and gazes out the window. That's when I start singing my best songs. It's my way of wishing him a good day.

I enjoyed watching him even before he was proclaimed Pope. He used to walk to work early in the morning, hurrying across the square. In the evening on his way home, he'd take his time and stop to shop in the small grocery stores in the Borgo Pio neighborhood. During the day, I'd see him on the streets of the Vatican or in his office. Back then, he was almost always alone. Now that he's Pope, however, he's always surrounded by many people.

The only time he's alone is when he's working at his large desk lit by a lamp shaped like the neck of those vain flamingos in the Villa Borghese Park.

I really like Benedict, also because he is a little like me. For example, I think he's a bit shy, and he likes his privacy. Some might mistake that for coolness or, in my case, sadness. But it's not like that at all.

People often visit the dome to see the view, and sometimes I overhear them comparing Benedict and the previous Pope. That's silly: they're two unique and very different people. It would be like comparing me to one of those gray herons you see on the Tiber River. They're so beautiful: when they spread their wings, it almost seems as if they're embracing the sky. I don't look so spectacular when I spread my wings, and I certainly can't fly like a gray heron. But few can top my singing. When I start, believe me, everyone stops to listen.

 "Hey, did you hear that blue bird sing?" they say.

"So sweet! Such a heartfelt sound!"

When they go home, my song still echoes in their ears . . . and they never forget it.

"How did that little blue bird sing? Tweet! Tweet! Chirrrr!! I can still remember his tune. His singing really touched me."

I might not be as grand as a heron, but I'm full of surprises, too!

In fact, I'm sure you'll be surprised by the story I'm about to tell.

I left my favorite spot on the dome to come here to tell you how Benedict spends his days and what he does. His job is very special and full of responsibility.

It's an exhausting job. I know, because I watch Benedict from morning to night.

His day starts at dawn. The lights in his apartment switch on when I'm still blinking, trying to wake up. While I shake my wings a bit and start grooming my feathers, wiggling my feet a little after spending the night standing on just one leg, Benedict is already preparing to say Mass. He prays in a small chapel with his family, which isn't his "real" family—not like yours—but the people who help him each day: his two secretaries, for example, the cook who prepares delicious apple strudel for him, the person who takes care of his clothes, and so on. In the Vatican, they say these people are the Pope's family.

Speaking of families, did you know that the Pope loves families like yours? He never tires of speaking of them, and he always reminds us how important families are and how we must protect them from people who don't recognize their value.

Birds have always appreciated the value of families, which is why we protect ours with lion-like courage. You should see me when someone approaches the nest made of leaves and moss where my darling wife is raising our babies: you had better stay out of my way! In tough moments, I'm as courageous as a kestrel, which even fights much larger peregrine falcons when it has to protect its family.

After Mass, around 8:00 A.M., the Pope goes to his study. First, he checks his mail and reads the most interesting newspaper articles. Afterwards, he concentrates on the documents that his two secretaries bring him. You have no idea how many things he must read each day! But that's understandable because all aspects of the Catholic Church, from every corner of the world, end up on his desk.

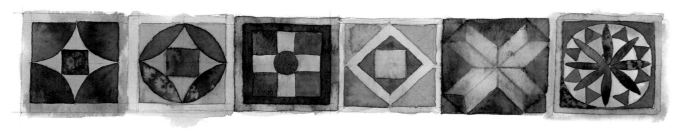

He has to deal with various problems that must be solved, and he must also sign official documents. That's when he takes his fountain pen and writes in teeny tiny letters: *Benedictus PP XVI.*

Some of the speeches that he wrote a few days earlier and will be presenting that day are also among those sheets of paper. He carefully checks them because everyone will be listening to each word. Benedict calmly rereads everything and doesn't like to rush.

Benedict's dearest friends are the many books in the room, and he often consults them whenever any doubts arise. Benedict leaves his desk around 10:30 A.M. because it is time for his private audiences, in which he welcomes official visitors. If we were comparing these visitors to my feathered friends, they would be birds of all types, from hummingbirds to ostriches. But since we're talking about humans, I can tell you that he meets all sorts of people who speak about major matters involving whole countries or small episodes referring to particular personal cases.

Benedict enjoys welcoming cardinals and bishops arriving from every corner of the earth. He has long conversations with them about their work and concerns; he listens to them with great interest and offers advice.

When he meets people who rule other countries, he always talks about peace, freedom, and justice. He also speaks about our duty to fight poverty. He reminds people that they must respect life and nature, which are wonderful gifts of God.

Important persons of other religions often come to visit. With them, Benedict always speaks about tolerance, which is an important word that means having respect for other people's ideas, and cooperation for the good of mankind.

Sometimes he meets with people who have gone through terrible experiences. Other times, he meets with associations, athletes, and celebrities. He always has the right word for the situation and a gentle smile.

The guests almost always bring a gift to express their gratitude—usually, books, paintings, medals, or religious objects. Sometimes, though, rather odd things arrive, such as the steering wheel of a Formula One race car with the inscription "To His Holiness Benedict XVI—the driver of Christianity". He even received a white tractor and a precious sculpture of a camel underneath a palm tree! In these cases, he is a bit surprised, but he always warmly thanks the giver because each gift was prepared with much love.

You might be wondering how I know all this. Well, I'll admit I'm a very curious blue rock-thrush! So when I go hunting for bugs on the windowsills of the rooms where the meetings are held, I always stop to watch and listen to what is going on inside.

I really enjoy observing the people waiting to meet Benedict. They're always so nervous! Some keep adjusting their ties, others smooth their hair, and some adjust the crosses hanging from their necks. Some people rock back and forth on their feet. Others check their shoes to see if they're polished. Still others quietly go over their speech to the Pope. . . .

During the meetings, things calm down because Benedict is so down-to-earth and kind that everyone immediately feels at ease. He kindly looks into their eyes and carefully listens to them, and then he affectionately clasps their hands as he speaks to them calmly. And sometimes he even adds a touch of humor in his talks. Don't get me wrong: he doesn't tell one joke after another, but he sees the amusing aspects of life and likes to share them with people.

Speaking of fun, did you know that birds like to have fun, too? In our own way, of course. If I want to have a laugh, for example, I go to the Villa Borghese Park where sly gray crows drop the nuts they want to eat from high above to crack the shells on the asphalt lanes below. Sometimes, though, the nuts don't make it to the asphalt and end up hitting the head of someone passing by. You should see the look on the faces of these people when they're hit!

Every Wednesday, Benedict has a special appointment in Saint Peter's Square—the "public audience". Anyone can attend and greet the Pope . . . at a distance, of course! Otherwise, the Pope would be overwhelmed by the thousands of people who arrive and would like to shake his hand or even hug him before they listen to his simple yet profound speeches.

When the weather is bad, the audience is held indoors in a huge auditorium that is still unfortunately not large enough to hold everyone who would like to attend. Each time, so many people arrive that there isn't enough room for everyone indoors, so Benedict does his best to meet everyone outside, even if it's raining or cold.

When the audience is held outdoors, I never miss a minute. I'm lucky because I always have a front-row seat!

Benedict arrives aboard his white Popemobile amid the applause and cheers of the crowd.

"Be-ne-det-to, Be-ne-det-to!" they chant and applaud from every corner.

Before he takes his place, he travels past the crowd as the flashes on cameras keep going off.

It almost looks like a pop star arriving at his concert!

For such a shy and reserved person, it must not have been easy for him to become accustomed to these situations.

During the audience, Benedict sits under a huge canopy in front of the basilica. Sometimes, when it is very hot or very cold, I feel so bad for him having to sit still for two hours: teaching, reading, and greeting the crowd. He doesn't seem to mind, though.

When he begins his speech, silence falls over the square. Everyone wants to hear him talk about Jesus and His love for us all, and the importance of trying to behave like Christ in our daily lives.

Benedict's simple words are always strong and clear, and they touch the hearts of his listeners.

When he speaks, a pair of herring gulls often circles the canopy. I know those two: they're bossy birds convinced they own the square. They usually stand on the head of one of the statues decorating the colonnade, and they're always ready to swoop down when they see something they can gobble up on the ground. During the audiences, however, there's no room for their raids because so many people have filled the square and are listening to the Pope. So the two birds are forced to postpone their food hunt, and they cheer themselves up by playfully chasing each other in the sky. I'm not very fond of those birds, but I have to admit that watching them glide and soar is a great spectacle. Even Benedict watches them sometimes. Who knows? Maybe he's thinking of how a bird's life is so wonderful and free. The second part of the audience is the official moment for greeting the crowd.

Because the crowd is so huge, even if he would like to, the Pope can't personally greet everyone who has come.

Imagine what would happen if he tried:

"Greetings to Pola and Wladyslaw, who came from Zielona Gòra!"

"Hello to Matthew, who came all the way from San Francisco!"

"Greetings to Teresa, from Madrid!"

"Hello, Georg, from Vienna!"

"Greetings to Tobias, who came from Padua!" No, he certainly couldn't do that!

At the end of the audience, he only mentions the large groups of people who informed him in advance of their presence, and he greets them in their own language. Every time he says the name of a particular group of pilgrims, you hear a great cheer "Yaaaaa!" and applause. He waves to them as if they were old friends. At the end of the audience, Benedict solemnly and affectionately blesses everyone. It is a small but very important gift from the Pope that everyone appreciates and will never forget.

Before he leaves the square, Benedict stops to greet the people standing next to the canopy, and he receives the gifts they brought him. Sometimes he comes across things that are a bit odd for a Pope, such as a football jersey with the name "Benedict" and the number 16, a portable pizza oven, a traffic cop's little notebook for fines, a racing bike, and so on. In each instance, he smiles and fondly thanks the donor.

Occasionally, there's a special blessing at the end of the audience. Some time ago, he blessed the new fire truck for Vatican firefighters. He even blessed four chickens with tufts on their heads. Actually, he blessed all the people who brought them, but the birds were at the center of the scene, so they were blessed, too! It was a delightful, amusing moment, even though the four chickens clucked a little too loud for my tastes. Now they live in the gardens of the Pope's summer home.

Benedict returns to his apartment around 1:00 P.M. and has a simple, light lunch. Afterwards, he goes for a stroll on the terraces above the apostolic palace where he lives. No one can see him from Saint Peter's Square, but I often follow him as I fly from one wall to another. He walks briskly, but always looks relaxed and calm.

Duty soon calls. I would really love for him to stay there and enjoy his stroll; I could even sing a bit for him. However, he must return to his study before 3:00 P.M., because much work awaits him. He has to read many documents and letters, write speeches and messages, correct texts, and delegate tasks.

He sometimes writes special letters called "encyclicals". This strange word comes from ancient Greek, an old language like Latin, that no one speaks anymore. Encyclical means "circular letter". The Pope sends these letters to Catholics around the world to speak of things he cares about deeply, such as God's love. That is the greatest love of all, because God *is* Love.

Well, these letters aren't mailed to absolutely everyone. Could you imagine how many stamps his secretaries would have to stick on the envelopes?

"What point are we at now?"

"We just finished the letter F in Australia."

"Great! We only have nine hundred and seventy million, five hundred and twenty four thousand more!"

It would be impossible to send these encyclical letters to everyone. They are sent to bishops, printed in books sold in bookstores, published in newspapers, and placed on the Internet. That way, everyone can read them. The encyclicals are somewhat long and are an important part of the history of the Church. Each Pope is also remembered for the encyclicals that he has written, so preparing them requires quite a lot of effort.

Benedict takes a break at 4:00 P.M. He goes for another stroll in the Vatican Gardens to relax and to stretch his legs.

Have you heard of these gardens? They're wonderful: a true paradise for us birds. In fact, thousands of birds live there. There are so many birds flying around above the treetops that you almost need floating traffic lights!

Small bright green parakeets—monk parakeets and ring-necked parakeets—are the noisiest birds that cause all the traffic jams in the sky. Once these birds only lived in countries with tropical climates, but now they can also be found in parks in Rome where certain types of exotic plants grow.

I often follow Benedict during his strolls in the garden, especially in the fall when I can find my favorite berries on ivy, strawberry trees, myrtle, and laurel trees. Sometimes there are so many that I don't know where to begin!

In the upper part of the garden, I always find a few tiny firecrests and some bizarre creepers, which hunt upside-down on tree trunks, looking for insects. There are also groups of greenfinches, European serins, and great tits—birds that love to gobble up acorns. There's a smart European nuthatch in the woods that uses mud to make holes in trees smaller to protect the place where he makes his nest. It's interesting to watch him work.

If I hear cackling, I know the green woodpecker has arrived from the countryside. These woodpeckers are so silly: it always seems they're laughing out loud. They never used to visit the city, but now they spend long periods in this part of town.

What I really enjoy doing in the Vatican gardens is to stand—sorry, I mean, perch—on an eagle's head. I do it every time I go there. I told you that I'm a very special bird! Here's what I do: I sneak up on that big nasty eagle, I land on its head, and I perch there and look around. Then I hop onto its beak and casually stroll up and down its open wings. What fun! The eagle never opens its beak and lets me do exactly as I please. It knows I'm a *very* special bird. Um . . . er . . . well, to tell the truth, it's a stone eagle at the top of a fountain. There are no real eagles here, and if there were, well, I'd keep out of their way. I'm a solitary blue rock-thrush, not a stupid one!

The Pope and his secretaries walk briskly, reciting the Rosary. They always stop to pray in front of the Madonna of Lourdes grotto, which is covered in the warmer months by a climbing vine that is home to a nest of wrens. There's even the titmouse, which loves to perch in front of this grotto. While Benedict takes his walk, I fly off for a snack and also go to see who's in the area. Sometimes, I meet up with relatives who live on the walls of Vatican Boulevard. My relatives are quiet loners, too, so we don't waste too much time chatting:

"Hello!"

"Hi!"

"How's everything?"

"Fine, thanks. How about you?"

"Fine. The usual stuff . . ."

"Great! See you!"

"Bye bye!"

I leave the garden when Benedict and his secretaries go indoors. I wouldn't want to find myself beak to beak with one of those tawny owls that always hunt at night. They're very aggressive birds, so it's best to stay out of their way.

The Pope is back at his desk before 5:00 P.M. He often devotes this part of his day to his books—the ones he writes. Benedict loves to write as much as he loves to read. He's always happy when he is preparing a book, even if writing is a very difficult job because you have to find the right words to explain different topics so everyone can understand. His books are a success around the world because—like the best teachers—he explains even difficult things in a very simple way.

The Pope receives other visits in the late afternoon: the cardinals in charge of the most important offices of the Vatican come to inform Benedict of their work and to ask for advice on certain problems.

Finally, at dusk, the time has come for some relaxation, even for the Pope! After a light, simple dinner (you could say he eats like a bird!), he watches the news on TV and then he relaxes with a book or some music.

In the evening, I return to my safe little cranny on the dome that I call home. From there, I can still hear Benedict when he sits at the piano and decides to play something before going to bed. He's a fine pianist, and I would really enjoy singing with him one day.

Benedict loves music. He enjoys a good concert whenever he can, but he doesn't have too much free time because his days are always so full of appointments and things to do.

Benedict never stops working, even when he's on holiday. How do I know? Easy! Sometimes I follow the helicopter that takes him to Castel Gandolfo, the summer residence of the Popes, so I've seen how he spends his days there.

Well, it was a surprise! It's not much of a vacation, because Benedict is as busy there as he is in Rome! He has audiences, letters to write, documents to read, speeches to prepare, meetings, and papers to sign. He spends much time on the new books he is writing. He's lucky if he finds a few minutes to go for a nice walk in the park where, among the many birds, there are also long-tailed titmice, Sardinian warblers, and a few robins.

When he has the time, Benedict sits at the piano to play something. My cousin, who lives on top of the clock on the front of Castel Gandolfo, told me that when the windows are open in the evening, the air fills with sweet music that lulls the birds to sleep in nearby nests.

At noon every Sunday, whether he's at Castel Gandolfo or in Rome, Benedict gives a short speech and then he recites the lovely Angelus prayer together with the people who have come to see him. It is an important moment because he mentions current problems and invites us to follow the teachings of Jesus to solve them. He also expresses his concerns for the bad things that happen around the world such as wars, violence against innocent people, and famine in the poorest countries.

I like to sit on the dome and observe Saint Peter's Square during the Angelus: it's so packed with people that sometimes you can't see an inch of pavement! When it's raining and the people have their umbrellas open, it seems as if a giant hand from above sprinkled colorful confetti all over the square.

Sometimes the square isn't large enough to contain all the people who have come to listen to the Pope. If they don't find room in the square, they have to stand in nearby streets to listen to Benedict's speech.

This mainly happens at Christmas and Easter, when Benedict says a magnificent Mass in the basilica full of candles, music, incense, and flowers. Numerous cardinals and bishops in their most elegant vestments also attend. Everything is breathtakingly beautiful and carefully prepared according to strict rules, like all great festivities. That's because celebrating Our Lord Jesus is always a wonderful occasion.

From my nice spot above the colonnade, I watch one of the large maxi-TV screens set up in the square. The best spot would be on top of the obelisk in the middle of the square, but I wouldn't feel comfortable surrounded by more than one hundred thousand people. Therefore, I like to hide way up high and watch everything that happens. I love watching Benedict on important occasions!

Due to the many things that he must do and the great number of people that he must meet, these special days are tiring for Benedict. Nevertheless, he happily welcomes these opportunities because he knows that his words and gestures help many people feel joyously closer to Jesus.

At the end of these High Masses, the Pope wishes the world a happy holiday, and he blesses everyone in sixty-three languages. Get that? Not three or four, but sixty-three! Your language, too. It takes him nearly thirty minutes to read all these messages, and I've heard that his pronunciation is very good. But do you know what language he speaks best? It's one that we can all speak perfectly: the language of love.

45

There are always many children like you in the basilica and square. Benedict is delighted to see them because young people are always in his thoughts. He considers you his little friends, and he always reminds everyone how important it is to protect you and help you grow up serene and loved. You should hear his harsh words when he criticizes people who do not respect children, who exploit them, and who even force them to be soldiers. There is no doubt about what he thinks.

Speaking of children, what meeting do you think was most extraordinary since Benedict was elected Pope? Can you guess?

Was it with a king? A football team? With highway patrol? With the tufted chickens? Noooo! It was with children—one hundred thousand children, to be precise. That's right: one hundred thousand! One-zero-zero-zero-zero-zero! It happened on October 15, 2005. On that Saturday afternoon, the Pope met with one hundred thousand children who just had or were about to have their First Holy Communion. It was a wonderful occasion, and I watched everything from above, on my perch. I had never seen anything like it on Saint Peter's Square. The children asked Benedict many questions, and he answered everything simply and clearly. To a child who asked how he could tell if Jesus was in the Communion Wafer because He couldn't be seen, Benedict gave a good explanation with a very original example: electricity. It's in everyone's home and makes the lights and appliances work, but we can't see it. It's the same with Jesus: *"We can't actually see Jesus with our eyes, but wherever He is, people change and become better persons. . . . Therefore, we can't see Jesus Himself, but we see His effects: that's how we know that Jesus is present."*

I think you'll agree with me now that the Pope is really a fascinating person. His work is extremely important for everyone, including all the children of the world.

So that's my story. Now I can fly up to my spot on the dome and see what Benedict is doing. Maybe he's getting ready for one of his official trips. Sometimes he travels far away to meet people who can't visit him in Rome. The trips are exhausting, but he loves them because he knows he will make many people smile and give them wonderful memories they'll never forget.

Of course, I can't follow him on those long trips, so I just wait here for him. When the shutters of his study are open, I know he's back. That's when I fly to the windowsill and start singing, Tweet! Tweet! Chirrrr!!

That's my way of saying, "Welcome home, dear Benedict! I missed you so much!"

Afterword

Birds fly. This fact might seem obvious, but except for the ostrich family, flying is a common characteristic of these extraordinary animals. Children's imaginations fly, too, and the imagination flies in every direction, without restraint. Authors of children's books cannot curb their imagination: on the contrary, they must stimulate and cultivate it. But being imaginative does not mean failing to provide factual information.

In this book, the author could have chosen any bird—a hummingbird, a parrot, a bird of paradise—but she chose a blue rock-thrush, a real bird of Rome and a species that makes its home in the ancient walls of Rome and the Vatican.

From high above the rooftops, this species has witnessed the splendors of ancient Rome, the barbarian invasions, famine and the plague, and periods of peace and war. It has also watched as men built the huge dome of Saint Peter's Basilica. The dome is a five-star residence for these birds: full of nooks, crannies, and ledges, it is the ideal place for a lifetime spent overlooking the city.

Rome is one of Europe's greenest cities. Wedges of Roman countryside reach the downtown area, right up to the Colosseum. Gardens with centuries-old trees interrupt the monotonous sequence of residential buildings, and among them are the Vatican Gardens. This urban park has attracted many birds, and more than seventy species have made it their home. In

51

the winter, many other birds arrive from the north to find hospitality in the mild city climate. These species, the co-stars of this story, actually live in Rome and the Vatican. Flying, they let our imaginations fly.

FULVIO FRATICELLI

Scientific Director, Biopark of Rome Foundation

Rome, January 27, 2009

*I am deeply grateful to Father Damiano Marzotto for the attention
that he has dedicated to my book project and my readers.*

*I am indebted to Fulvio Fraticelli, for introducing me to the marvelous
world of the birds of Rome.*

My thanks go to Giacomo dell'Omo for his fascinating stories of kestrels.

I am grateful to Maria Attinà [and Debbie Brumley] for fastidious proofreading.

*The Governorship of Vatican City State deserves a special note of thanks
for allowing me to explore the Vatican Gardens, and the Vatican Television Center
was an invaluable asset that allowed me to view many rare film documentaries.*

JEANNE PEREGO